Get The Ebook

Welcome to a world of colorful exploration! Each dot is a tiny adventure in learning, laughter, and love. Let's journey through these pages together, creating, discovering, and making memories with every dot

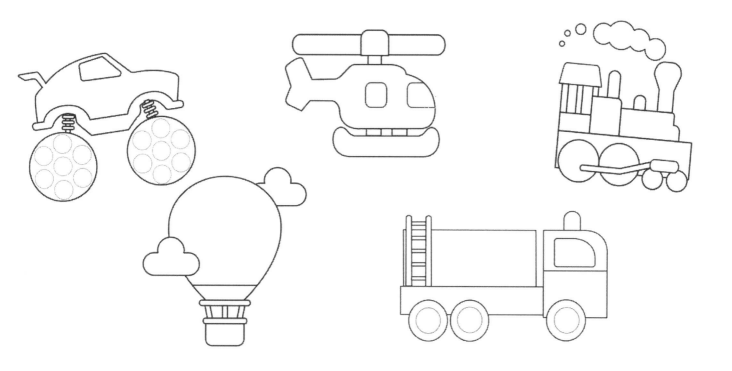

Art Adventures for Smart Minds!

For kids and grown-ups alike, coloring is like a super-fun brain workout that makes you smarter, happier, and super relaxed. Get your crayons ready for an amazing adventure in art that's not just awesome, but brain-boosting too!

Ink Bleeding and Paper Quality

We've selected standard quality paper for our coloring book to keep it affordable for everyone. Plus, we've made the back of each page black to help prevent ink from bleeding through. If you still notice some ink bleeding, just slip an extra sheet of paper behind the page to protect the next one. Happy coloring without the worry!

Share and Show your Artwork

For advance learner, you can follow the cutting lines on each of the pages to showcase your favorite masterpiece, We kindly ask you to keep a watchful eye and be present when those little hands are at work with scissors.

Share on your instagram or tiktok, and tagged us as well! We love to see your guys works! We also share tips and tricks on how to color and exiciting promos on upcoming books!

Also visit us at gentlewhisperstories.com or scan the qr below, and please write us a review on AMAZON if you love our book so we can reach more people!

or

drop a follow at

@kreative.ink.color

subscribe to us and contact for
free soft copy of your book!

THIS BOOK BELONG TO

○○

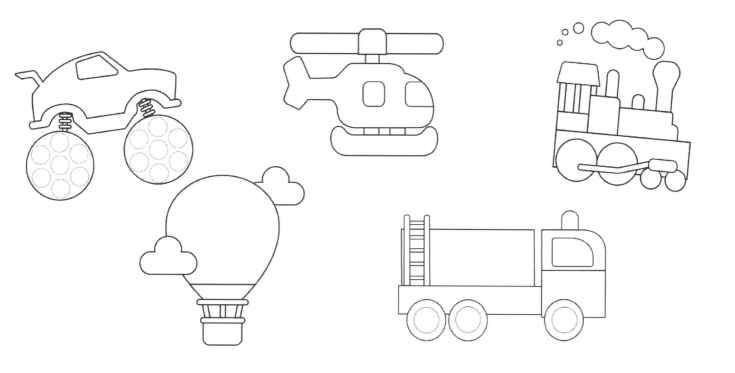

LET'S PRACTICE

CAT

Say it and Spell it :

c a t

Built it :

Trace it :

DOG

Say it and Spell it :

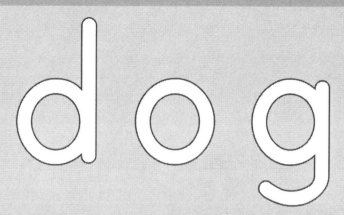

Built it :

Trace it :

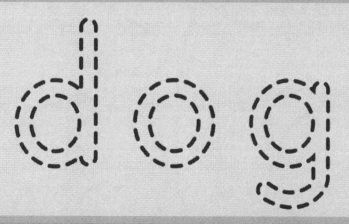

DUCK

Say it and Spell it :

duck

Built it :

Trace it :

duck

RABBIT

Say it and Spell it :

rabbit

Built it :

Trace it :

rabbit

BEAR

Say it and Spell it :

bear

Built it :

Trace it :

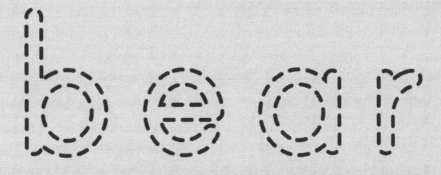

HORSE

Say it and Spell it :

horse

Built it :

Trace it :

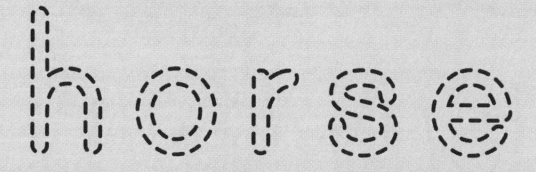

PANDA

Say it and Spell it :

p a n d a

Built it :

Trace it :

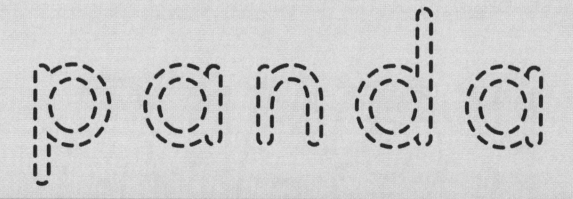

KOALA

Say it and Spell it :

koala

Built it :

Trace it :

koala

PENGUIN

Say it and Spell it :

penguin

Built it :

Trace it :

ELEPHANT

Say it and Spell it :

elephant

Built it :

Trace it :

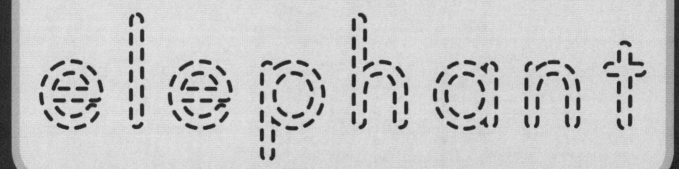

DOLPHIN

Say it and Spell it :

dolphin

Built it :

Trace it :

dolphin

TURTLE

Say it and Spell it :

turtle

Built it :

Trace it :

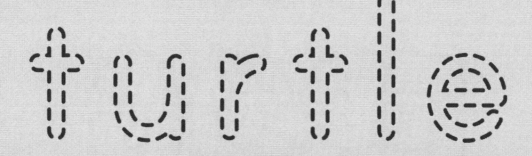

FROG

Say it and Spell it :

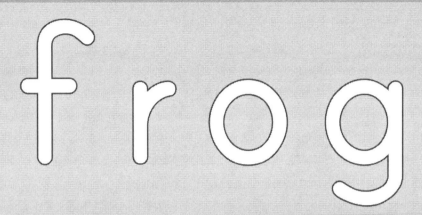

Built it :

Trace it :

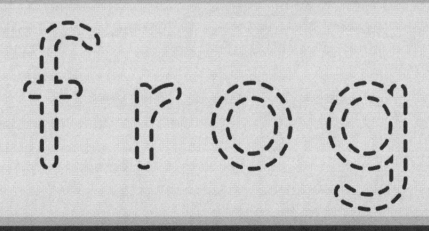

Say it and Spell it :

o w l

Built it :

Trace it :

LION

Say it and Spell it :

lion

Built it :

Trace it :

lion

SNAKE

Say it and Spell it :

snake

Built it :

Trace it :

Say it and Spell it :

jellyfish

Built it :

Trace it :

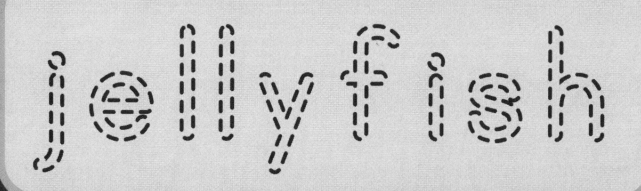

OCTOPUS

Say it and Spell it :

octopus

Built it :

Trace it :

HELLO

Hey there little artist!

Dear Parents and Little Artists,

Thank you for joining the colorful adventure within these pages! Your support means the world.

We hope these dot marker activities bring endless joy and creativity to your little one's world. Their imagination is a masterpiece in the making!

If this book brings smiles and giggles, we'd be honored if you could share your thoughts with a review on Amazon.

Your feedback helps other families discover the joy within these dots!

Thank you for being part of our colorful journey!

Much love,

Kreative Ink Team

scan here to get our latest update!

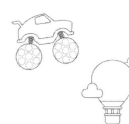

FAIRY

Say it and Spell it :

fairy

Built it :

Trace it :

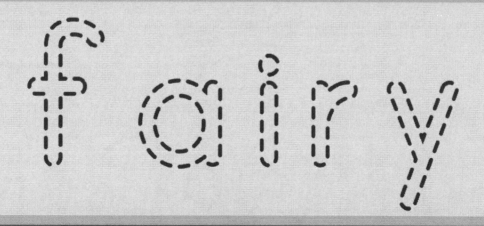

UNICORN

Say it and Spell it :

unicorn

Built it :

Trace it :

unicorn

MERMAID

Say it and Spell it :

mermaid

Built it :

Trace it :

mermaid

DRAGON

Say it and Spell it :

dragon

Built it :

Trace it :

dragon

SANTA

Say it and Spell it :

santa

Built it :

Trace it :

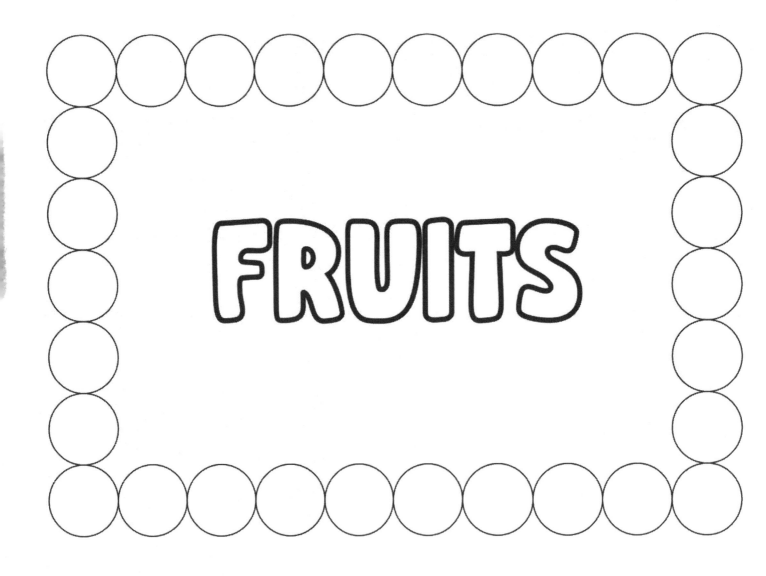

FRUITS

HELLO

Hey there little artist!

Dear Parents and Little Artists,

Thank you for joining the colorful adventure within these pages! Your support means the world.

We hope these dot marker activities bring endless joy and creativity to your little one's world. Their imagination is a masterpiece in the making!

If this book brings smiles and giggles, we'd be honored if you could share your thoughts with a review on Amazon.

Your feedback helps other families discover the joy within these dots!

Thank you for being part of our colorful journey!

Much love,

Kreative Ink Team

scan here to get our latest update!

GRAPES

Say it and Spell it :

grapes

Built it :

Trace it :

STRAWBERRY

Say it and Spell it :

strawberry

Built it :

Trace it :

strawberry

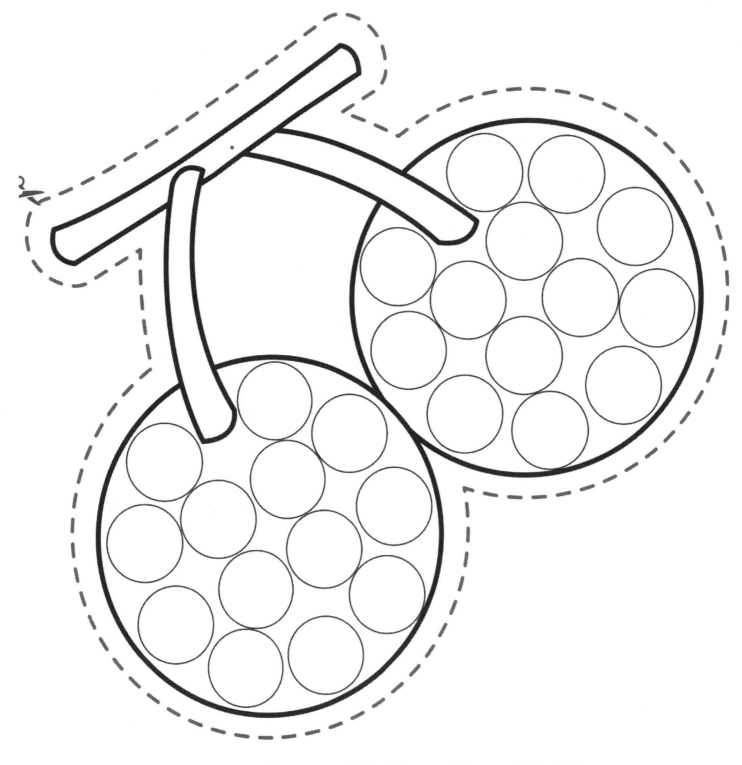

CHERRY

Say it and Spell it :

cherry

Built it :

Trace it :

cherry

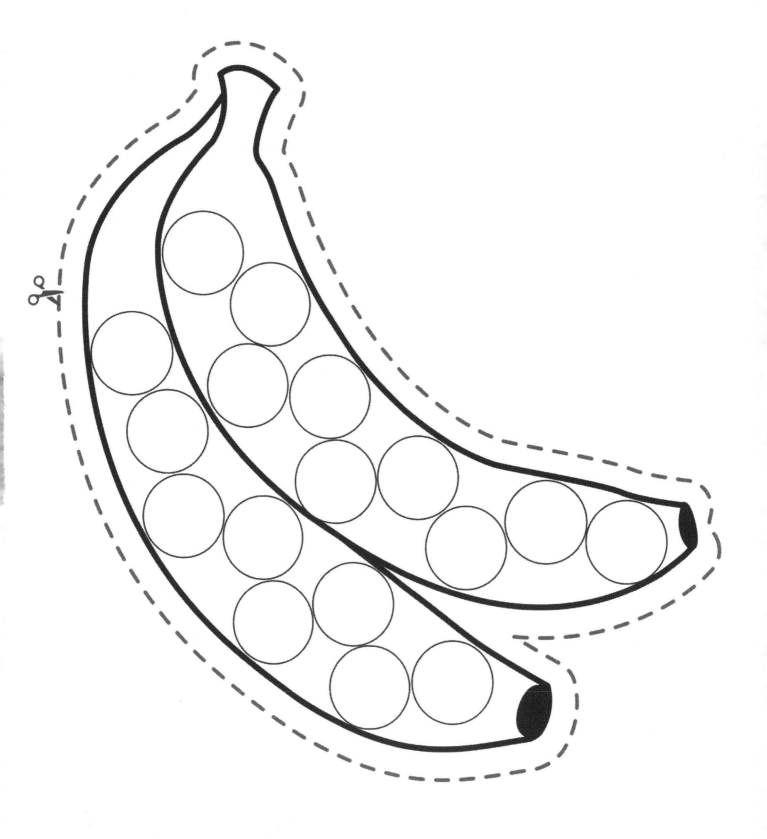

BANANA

Say it and Spell it :

banana

Built it :

Trace it :

banana

APPLE

Say it and Spell it :

apple

Built it :

Trace it :

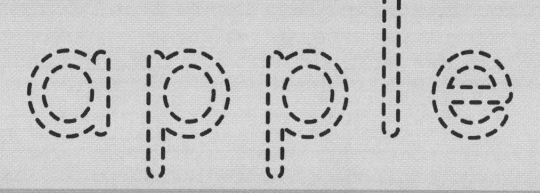

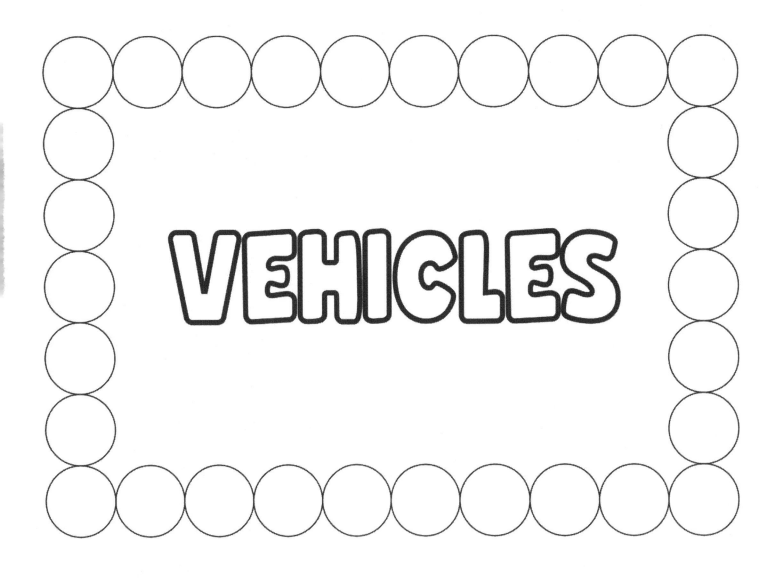

HELLO

Hey there little artist!

Dear Parents and Little Artists,

Thank you for joining the colorful adventure within these pages! Your support means the world.

We hope these dot marker activities bring endless joy and creativity to your little one's world. Their imagination is a masterpiece in the making!

If this book brings smiles and giggles, we'd be honored if you could share your thoughts with a review on Amazon.

Your feedback helps other families discover the joy within these dots!

Thank you for being part of our colorful journey!

Much love,

Kreative Ink Team

scan here to get our latest update!

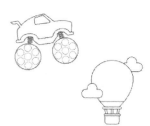

CAR

Say it and Spell it :

car

Built it :

Trace it :

FIRE TRUCK

Say it and Spell it :

fire truck

Built it :

Trace it :

fire truck

TRACTOR

Say it and Spell it :

tractor

Built it :

Trace it :

tractor

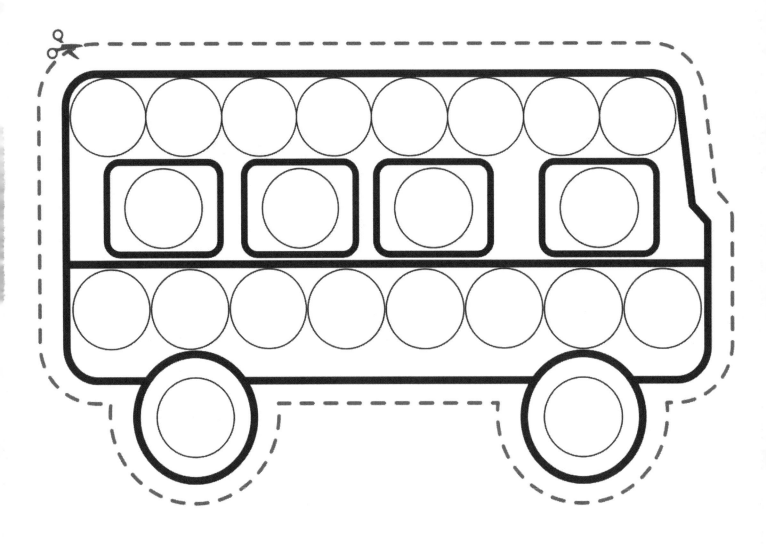

BUS

Say it and Spell it :

bus

Built it :

Trace it :

bus

ICE CREAM TRUCK

Say it and Spell it :

ice cream truck

Built it :

Trace it :

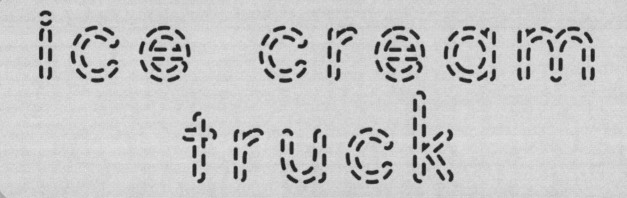

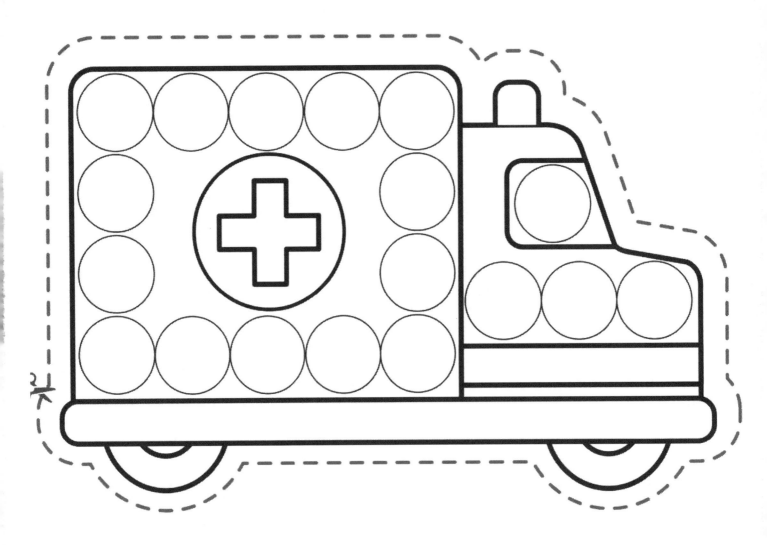

AMBULANCE

Say it and Spell it :

ambulance

Built it :

Trace it :

ambulance

POLICE CAR

Say it and Spell it :

police car

Built it :

Trace it :

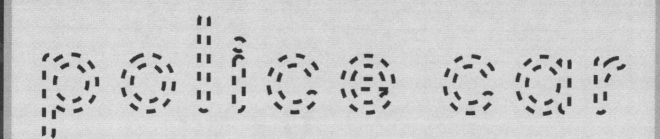

TRAIN

Say it and Spell it :

train

Built it :

Trace it :

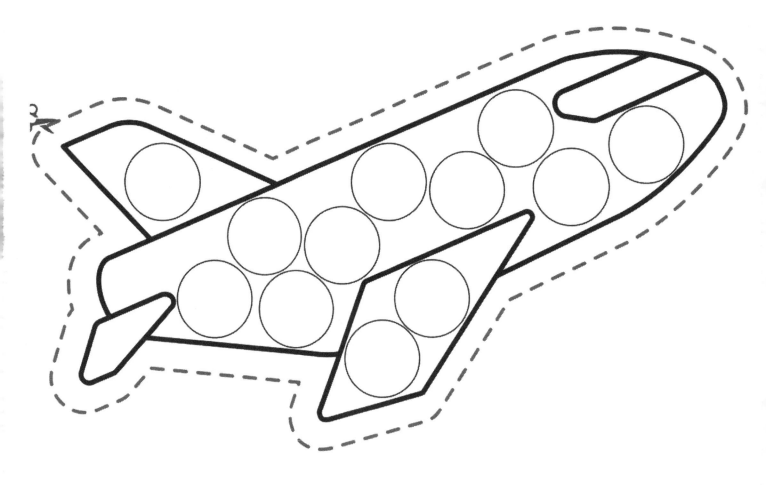

AIRPLANE

Say it and Spell it :

airplane

Built it :

Trace it :

airplane

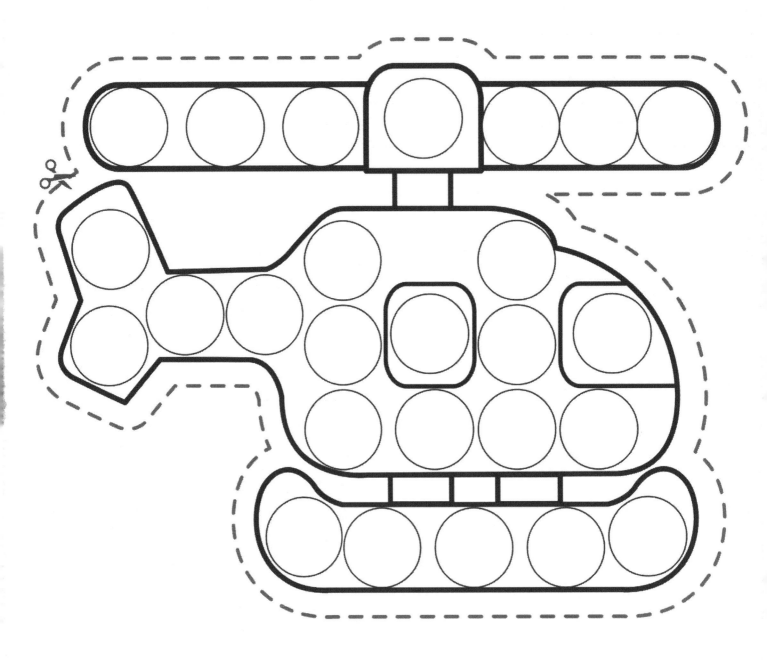

HELICOPTER

Say it and Spell it :

helicopter

Built it :

Trace it :

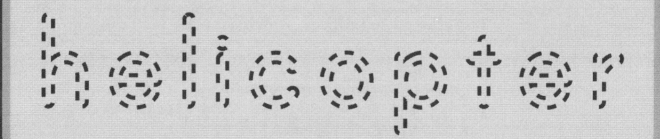

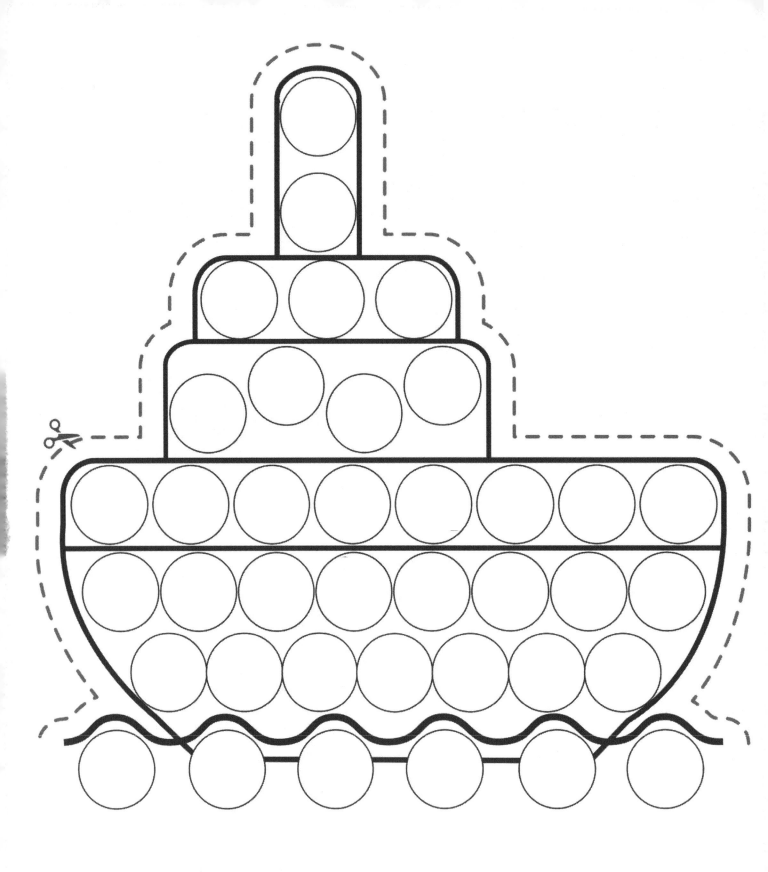

BOAT

Say it and Spell it :

b o a t

Built it :

Trace it :

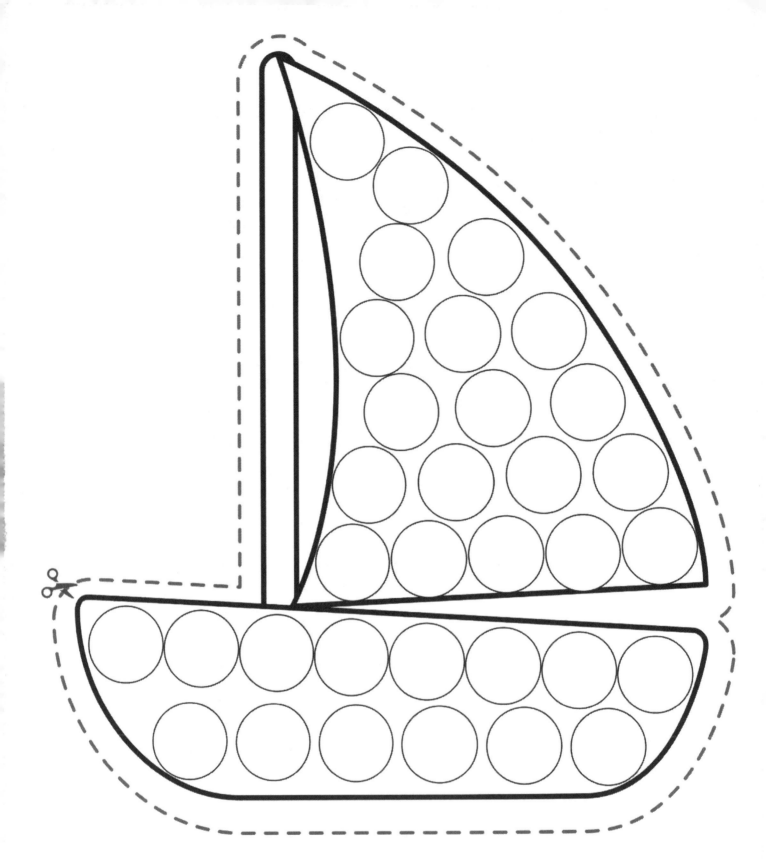

SAILBOAT

Say it and Spell it :

sailboat

Built it :

Trace it :

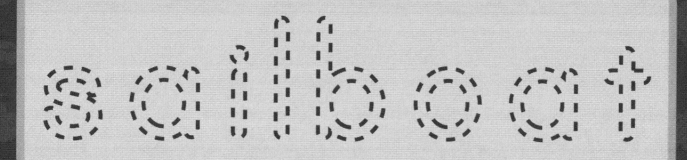

MOTORCYCLE

Say it and Spell it :

motorcycle

Built it :

Trace it :

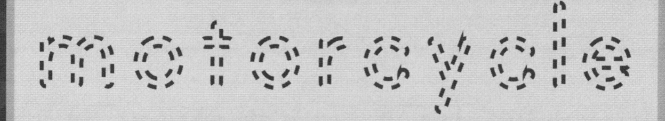

HOT AIR BALLOON

Say it and Spell it :

hot air balloon

Built it :

Trace it :

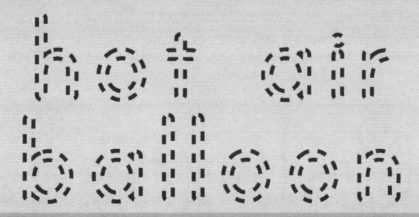

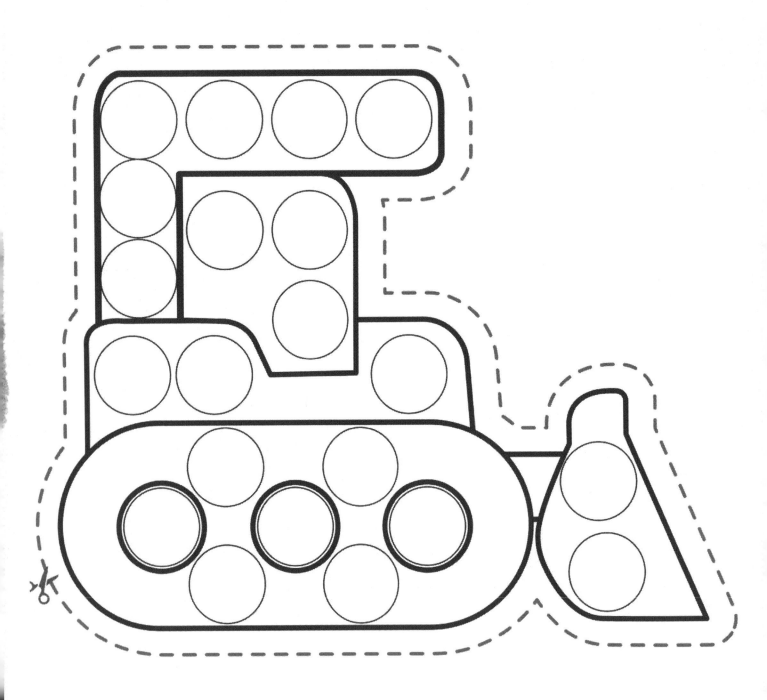

BULLDOZER

Say it and Spell it :

bulldozer

Built it :

Trace it :

bulldozer

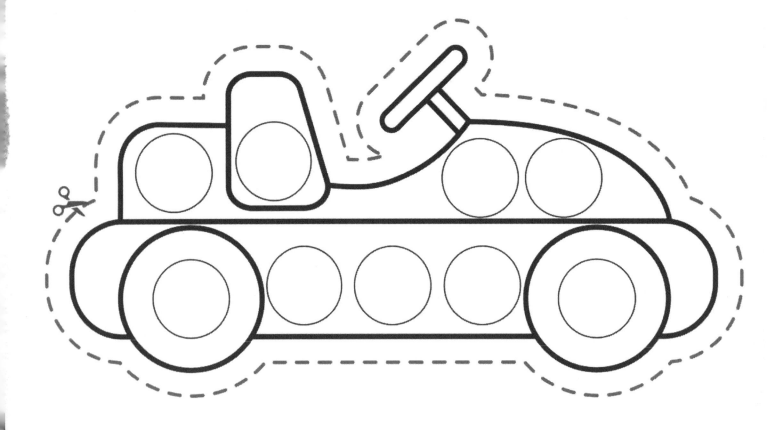

GO - KART

Say it and Spell it :

go-kart

Built it :

Trace it :

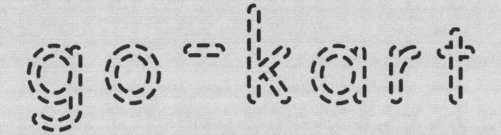

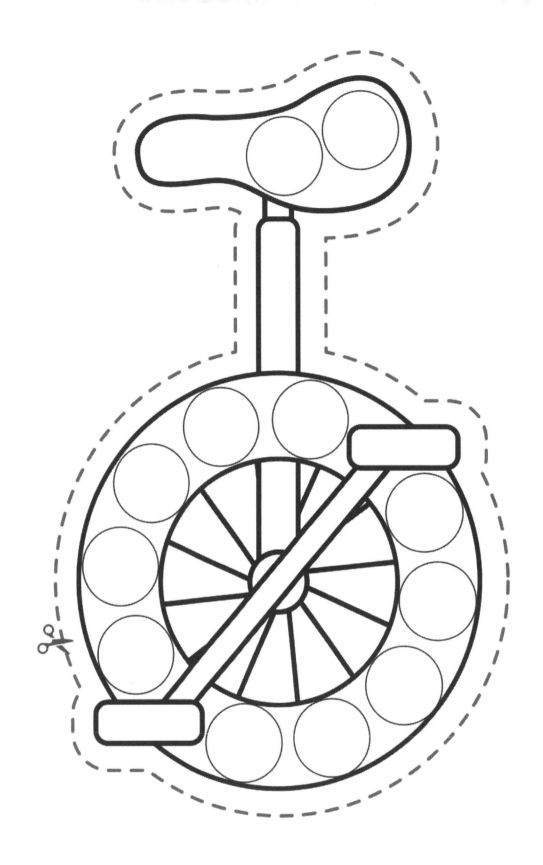

MONOCYCLE

Say it and Spell it :

monocycle

Built it :

Trace it :

monocycle

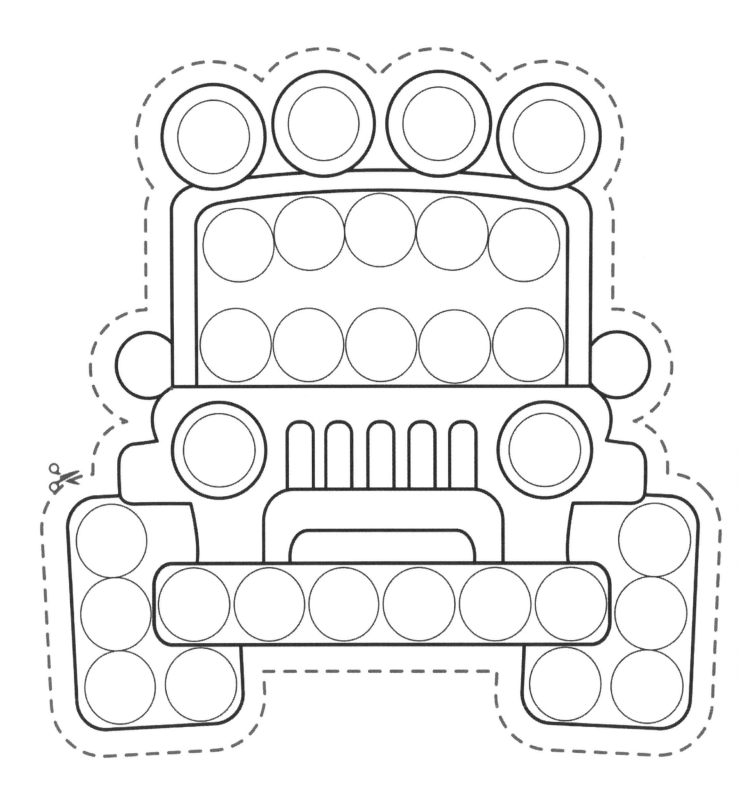

JEEP

Say it and Spell it :

jeep

Built it :

Trace it :

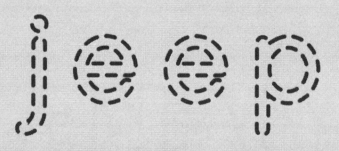

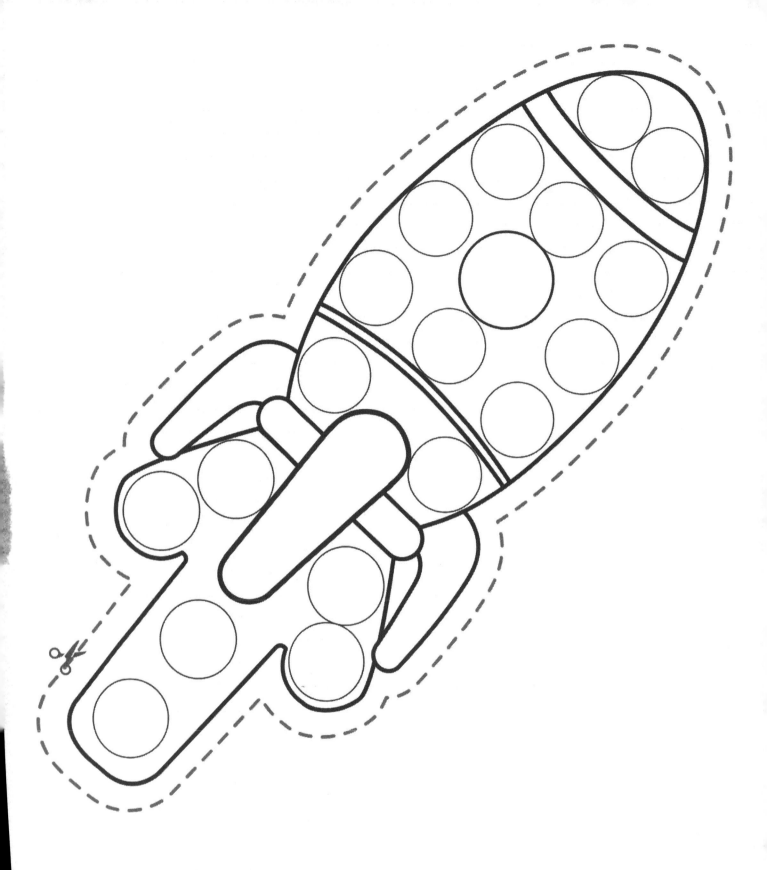

ROCKET

Say it and Spell it :

rocket

Built it :

Trace it :

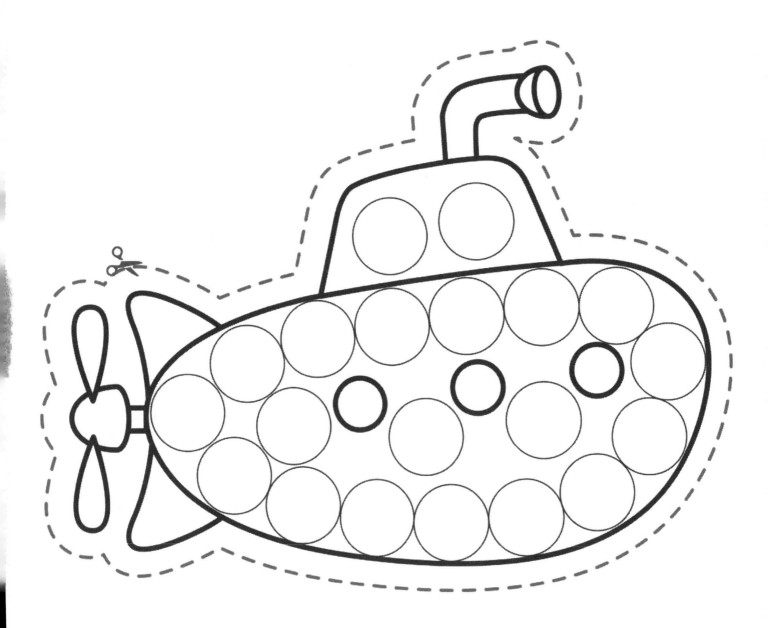

SUBMARINE

Say it and Spell it :

submarine

Built it :

Trace it :

submarine

MONSTER TRUCK

Say it and Spell it :

monster truck

Built it :

Trace it :

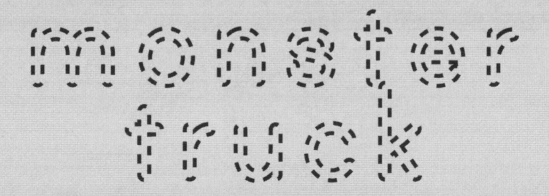

CONGRATULATION

Hey there little artist!

Dear Parents and Little Artists,

Great job finishing this book!!! You're AMAZING!!

Thank you for joining the colorful adventure within these pages! Your support means the world.

We hope these dot marker activities bring endless joy and creativity to your little one's world. Their imagination is a masterpiece in the making!

If this book brings smiles and giggles, we'd be honored if you could share your thoughts with a review on Amazon.

Your feedback helps other families discover the joy within these dots!

Thank you for being part of our colorful journey!

Much love,

Kreative Ink Team

scan here to get our latest update!

Made in the USA
Middletown, DE
27 September 2024

61541307R00064